The Elementary Spirit

By

E. T. A. Hoffmann

British Library Cataloguing-in-Publication Data
A catalogue record for this book is available from the
British Library

E. T. A. Hoffman

Ernst Theodor Wilhelm Hoffmann was born in Königsberg, East Prussia in 1776. His family were all jurists, and during his youth he was initially encouraged to pursue a career in law. However, in his late teens Hoffman became increasingly interested in literature and philosophy, and spent much of his time reading German classicists and attending lectures by, amongst others, Immanuel Kant.

In was in his twenties, upon moving with his uncle to Berlin, that Hoffman first began to promote himself as a composer, writing an operetta called Die Maske and entering a number of playwriting competitions. Hoffman struggled to establish himself anywhere for a while, flitting between a number of cities and dodging the attentions of Napoleon's occupying troops. In 1808, while living in Bamberg, he began his job as a theatre manager and a music critic, and Hoffman's break came a year later, with the publication of Ritter Gluck. The story centred on a man who meets, or thinks he has met, a long-dead composer, and played into the 'doppelgänger' theme – at that time very popular in literature. It was shortly after this that Hoffman began to use the pseudonym E. T. A. Hoffmann, declaring the 'A' to stand for 'Amadeus', as a tribute to the great composer, Mozart.

Over the next decade, while moving between Dresden, Leipzig and Berlin, Hoffman produced a great range of both literary and musical works. Probably Hoffman's most well-known story, produced in 1816, is 'The Nutcracker and the Mouse King', due to the fact that – some seventy-six years later - it inspired Tchaikovsky's ballet The Nutcracker.

In the same vein, his story 'The Sandman' provided both the inspiration for Léo Delibes's ballet Coppélia, and the basis for a highly influential essay by Sigmund Freud, called 'The Uncanny'. (Indeed, Freud referred to Hoffman as the "unrivalled master of the uncanny in literature.")

Alcohol abuse and syphilis eventually took a great toll on Hoffman though, and – having spent the last year of his life paralysed – he died in Berlin in 1822, aged just 46. His legacy is a powerful one, however: He is seen as a pioneer of both Romanticism and fantasy literature, and his novella, Mademoiselle de Scudéri: A Tale from the Times of Louis XIV is often cited as the first ever detective story.

The Elementary Spirit

On the 20th of November, 1815, Albert von B----, lieutenant-colonel in the Prussian service, found himself on the road from Liege to Aix-la-Chapelle. The corps to which he belonged was on its return from France to march to Liege to head-quarters on that very day, and was to remain there for two or three days more. Albert had arrived the evening before; but in the morning he felt himself attacked by a strange restlessness, and--as he would hardly have confessed to himself--an obscure dream, which had haunted him all night, and had foretold that a very pleasant adventure awaited him at Aix-la-Chapelle, was the only cause of his sudden departure. Much surprised even at his own proceeding, he was sitting on the swift horse, which would, he hoped, take him to the city before nightfall.

A severe cutting autumn wind roared over the bare fields, and awakened the voices of the leafless wood in the distance, which united their groans to its howling. Birds of prey came croaking, and followed in flocks the thick clouds which gathered more and more, until the last ray of sunlight had vanished, and a faint dull gray had overspread the entire sky. Albert wrapped his mantle more closely about him, and while he trotted on along the broad road, the picture of the last eventful time unfolded itself to his imagination. He thought how, a few months before, he had travelled on the same road, in an opposite direction, and during the loveliest season of the year. The fields then bloomed forth luxuriantly, the fragrant meadows resembled variegated carpets, and the bushes in which the birds joyously chirped and sung, shone in the fair light of golden sunbeams. The earth, like a longing bride, had richly adorned herself to receive in her dark nuptial chamber, the victims consecrated to death--the heroes who fell in the sanguinary battles.

Albert had reached the corps to which he was appointed, when the cannon had already begun to thunder by the Sambre, though he was in time enough to take part in the bloody battles of Charleroi, Gilly, and Gosselins. Indeed, chance seemed to wish that Albert should be present just when any thing decided took place. Thus he was at the last storming of the village Planchenoit, which caused the victory in the most remarkable of all battles--Waterloo. He was in the last engagement of the campaign, when the final effort of rage and fierce despair on the part of the enemy wreaked itself on the immoveable courage of the heroes, who having a fine position in the village of Issy, drove back the foe as they sought, amid the most furious discharge of grape, to scatter death and destruction in the ranks; and indeed drove them back so far, that the sharp-shooters pursued them almost to the barriers of Paris. The night afterwards (that of the 3rd and 4th of July), was, as is well known, that on which the military convention for the surrender of the metropolis was settled at St. Cloud.

The battle of Issy now rose brightly before Albert's soul; he thought of things, which as it seemed, he had not observed, nay, had not been able to observe during the fight.

Thus the faces of many individual officers and men appeared before his eyes, depicted in the most lively manner, and his heart was struck by the inexplicable expression, not of proud or unfeeling contempt of death, but of really divine inspiration, which beamed from many an eye. Thus he heard sounds, now exhorting to fight, now uttered with the last sigh of death, which deserved to be treasured up for posterity like the animating utterances of the heroes of antiquity.

"Do I not," thought Albert, "almost feel like one who has a notion of his dream when he wakes, but who does not recollect all its single features till several days afterwards? Ay, a dream, and only a dream, one would think, by flying over time and space, with its mighty wings, could render possible, the gigantic, monstrous, unheard-of events, that took place during the eighteen eventful days of a campaign, which mocks the boldest thoughts, the most daring combinations of the speculative mind. Indeed the human mind does not know its own greatness; the act surpasses the thought. For it is not rude physical force, no! it is the mind, which creates deeds as they have happened, and it is the psychic power of every single person, really inspired, which attaches itself to the wisdom and genius of the general, and helps to accomplish the monstrous and the unexpected."

Albert was disturbed in these meditations by his groom, who kept about twenty paces behind him, and whom he heard cry out, "Eh! Paul Talkebarth, where the deuce do you come from?" He turned his horse, and perceived that a horseman, who had just trotted past him, and whom he had not particularly observed, was standing still with his groom, beating out the cheeks of the large fox-fur cap with which his head was covered, so that soon the well-known face of Paul Talkebarth, Colonel Victor von S----'s old groom, was made manifest, glowing with the finest vermilion.

Now Albert knew at once what it was that impelled him so irresistibly from Liege to Aix-la-Chapelle, and he could not comprehend how the thought of Victor, his most intimate and dearest friend, whom he had every reason to suppose at Aix, merely lay dimly in his soul, and attained nothing like distinctness. He now also cried out, "Eh! Paul Talkebarth, whence do you come? Where is your master?"

Paul curvetted up to him very gracefully, and said, holding the palm of his hand against the far-too-large cockade of his cap, by way of military salutation: "Yes, 'faith, I am Paul Talkebarth indeed, gracious lieutenant-colonel. We've bad weather here, Zermannoere (sur mon honneur). But the groundsel brings that about. Old Lizzy always used to say so. I cannot say, gracious lieutenant-colonel, if you know Lizzy: she lives at Genthin, but if one has been at Paris, and has seen the wild goat in the Schartinpland (Jardin des Plantes).--Now, what one seeks for one finds near, and here I am in the presence of the gracious lieutenant-colonel, whom I was to seek at Liege. The spirus familis (spiritus familiaris), whispered yesterday evening into my master's ear, that the gracious lieutenant-colonel had come to Liege. Zackermannthoe (sacre mon de Dieu), there was delight! It may be as it will, but I have never put any faith in the cream-colour. A fine beast, Zermannoere, but a mere childish thing, and the baroness did her utmost--that is true! There are decent sort of people here, but the wine is good for nothing--and when one has been in Paris--! Now, the colonel might have marched in, like one through the Argen trumph (Arc de triomphe), and I should have put the new shabrach on the white horse; gad, how he would have pricked up his ears! But old Lizzy,--she was my aunt, at Genthin, was always accustomed to say--I don't know, gracious lieutenant-colonel, whether you--"

"May your tongue be lamed," said Albert, interrupting the incorrigible babbler. "If your master is at Aix, we must make haste, for we have still above five leagues to go."

"Stop," cried Paul Talkebarth, with all his might; "stop, stop, gracious lieutenant-colonel, the weather is bad here; but for fodder--those who have eyes like us, that shine in the fog."

"Paul," cried Albert, "do not wear out my patience. Where is your master? Is he not in Aix?"

Paul Talkebarth smiled with such delight, that his whole countenance puckered up into a thousand folds, like a wet glove, and then stretching out his arm he pointed to the building, which might be seen behind the wood, upon a gentle declivity, and said, "Yonder, in the castle!" Without waiting for what Paul might have to prattle further, Albert struck into the path that led from the high road, and hurried on in a rapid trot. After the little that he has said, honest Paul Talkebarth must appear to the gracious reader as an odd sort of fellow. We have only to say, that he being an heir-loom of the family, served Colonel Victor von S---- from the moment when the latter first put on his officer's sword, after having been the intendent-general and maitre des plaisirs of all the sports and mad pranks of his childhood. An old and very odd magister, who had been tutor to the family through two generations, completed, with the amount of education which he allowed to flow to honest Paul, those happy talents for extraordinary confusion and strange Eulenspiegelei[1] with which nature had by no means scantily endued him. At the same time he was the most faithful soul that could possibly exist. Ready every moment to sacrifice his life for his master, neither his advanced age nor any other consideration could prevent the good Paul from following him to the field in the year 1813. His own nature rendered him superior to every hardship; but less strong than his corporeal was his spiritual nature, which seemed to have received a strange shock, or at any rate some extraordinary impulse during his residence in France, especially in Paris. Then, for the first time, did he properly feel that Magister Spreugepileus had been perfectly right when he called him a great light, that would one day shine forth brightly. This shining quality Paul had discovered by the aptness with which he had accommodated himself to the manners of a foreign people, and had learned their language. Therefore, he boasted not a little, and ascribed it to his extraordinary talent alone, that he could often, in respect to quarters and provisions, obtain that which seemed unattainable. Talkebarth's fine French phrases, the gentle reader has already been made acquainted with some pleasant curses--were current, if not through the whole army, at any rate through the corps to which his master was attached. Every trooper who came to quarters in a village, cried to the peasant with Paul's words, "Pisang! de lavendel pur di schevals!" (Paysan, de l'avoine pour les chevaux.)

Paul, as is generally the case with eccentric natures, did not like things to happen in the ordinary manner. He was particularly fond of surprises, and sought to prepare them in every possible manner for his master, who was certainly often surprised, though in quite another manner than was designed by honest Talkebarth, whose happy schemes generally failed in their execution. Thus, he now entreated Lieutenant-colonel von B----, when the latter was riding straight up to the principal entrance of the house, to take a circuitous course and enter the court-yard by the back way, that his master might not see him before he entered the room. To meet this view, Albert was obliged to ride over a marshy meadow, where he was grievously splashed by the mud, and then he had to go over a fragile bridge on a ditch. Paul Talkebarth wished to show off his horsemanship by jumping cleverly over; but he fell in with his horse up to the belly, and was with difficulty brought back to firm ground by Albert's groom. Now, in high spirits, he put spurs to his horse, and with a wild huzza leaped into the court-yard. As all the geese, ducks, turkeys, and poultry of the household were gathered together here to rest; while from the one side a flock of sheep, and from the other side a flock of pigs, had been driven in, we may easily imagine that Paul Talkebarth, who not being perfect master of his horse, galloped about the court in large circles, without any will of his own, produced no little devastation in the domestic economy. Amid the fearful noise of squeaking, cackling, bleating, grunting animals, the barking of the dogs, and the scolding of the servants, Albert made his glorious entrance, wishing honest Paul Talkebarth at all the devils, with his project of surprise.

At last Albert leaped from his horse, and entered the house, which, without any claim to beauty or elegance, looked roomy and convenient enough. On the steps he was met by a well-fed, not very tall man, in a short, gray, hunting-jacket, who, with a half-sour smile, said: "Quartered?" By the tone in which the man asked this question, Albert perceived at once that the master of the house, Baron von E---- (as he had learned from Paul) was before him. He assured him that he was not quartered, but merely purposed to visit his intimate friend, Colonel Victor von S----, who was, he was told, residing there, and that he only required the baron's hospitality for that evening and the night, as he intended to start very early on the following morning.

The baron's face visibly cleared up, and the full sun-shine, which ordinarily seemed to play upon his good-humoured, but somewhat too broad, countenance, returned completely, when Albert as he ascended the stairs with him remarked, that in all probability no division of the army now marching would touch this spot.

The baron opened a door, Albert entered a cheerful-looking parlour, and perceived Victor, who sat with his back towards him. At the sound of his entrance Victor turned round, and with a loud exclamation of joy fell into the arms of the lieutenant. "Is it not true, Albert, you thought of me last night? I knew it, my inner sense told me that you were in Liege at the very moment when you first entered the place. I fixed all my thoughts upon you, my spiritual arms embraced you; you could not escape me."

Albert confessed that--as the gentle reader already knows--dark dreams which came to no clear shape had driven him from Liege.

"Yes," cried Victor, with transport, "yes, it is no fancy, no idle notion; the divine power is given to us, which, ruling space and time, manifests the supersensual in the world of sense."

Albert did not know what Victor meant. Indeed the whole behaviour of his friend, so different from his usual manner, seemed to denote an over-excited state. In the meanwhile the lady, who had been sitting before the fire near Victor, arose and approached the stranger. Albert bowed to her, casting an inquiring glance at Victor. "This is the Baroness Aurora von E----," said Victor, "my hospitable hostess, who tends me ever carefully and faithfully in sickness and in trouble!"

Albert as he looked at the baroness felt quite convinced that the little plump woman had not yet attained her fortieth year, and that she would have been very well made had not the nutritious food of the country, together with much sunshine, caused her shape to deviate a little from the line of beauty.

This counteracted the favourable effect of her pretty, fresh-coloured face, the dark blue eyes of which might otherwise have beamed somewhat dangerously for the heart. Albert considered the attire of the baroness almost too homely, for the material of her dress, which was of a dazzling whiteness, while it showed the excellence of the washing and bleaching department, also showed the great distance at which the domestic spinning and weaving stood from perfection. A cotton kerchief, of a very glaring pattern, thrown negligently about the neck, so that its whiteness was visible enough, did not at all increase the brilliant effect of the costume. The oddest thing of all was, that the baroness wore on her little feet the most elegant silken shoes, and on her head the most charming lace cap, after the newest Parisian fashion. This head-dress, it is true, reminded the lieutenant-colonel of a pretty grisette, with whom chance had made him acquainted at Paris, but for this very reason a quantity of uncommonly gallant things flowed from his lips, while he apologised for his sudden appearance. The baroness did not fail to reply to these prettinesses in the proper style, and having once opened her mouth the stream of her discourse flowed on uninterruptedly, till she at last went so far as to say, that it would be impossible to show sufficient attention to such an amiable guest, the friend of the colonel, who was so dear to the family. At the sudden ring of the bell, and the shrill cry: "Mariane, Mariane!" a peevish old woman made her appearance, who, by the bunch of keys which hung from her waist, seemed to be the housekeeper. A consultation was now held with this lady and the husband, as to what nice things could be got ready. It was soon found, however, that all the delicacies, such as venison and the like, were either already consumed, or could only be got the next day. Albert, with difficulty suppressing his displeasure, said, that they would force him to quit immediately in the night, if on his account they disturbed the arrangements of the house in the slightest degree. A little cold meat, nay, some bread and butter, would be sufficient for his supper. The baroness replied by protesting that it was impossible for the lieutenant-colonel to do without something warm, after his ride in the rough, bleak weather, and after a long consultation with Mariane, the preparation of some mulled wine was found to be possible and decided on. Mariane vanished through the door-way, rattling as she went, but at the very moment when they were about to take their seats, the baroness was called out by an amazed maid-servant. Albert overheard that the baroness was being informed at the door of the frightful devastations of Paul Talkebarth, with a list--no inconsiderable one--of the dead, wounded, and missing. The baron ran out after his wife, and while she was scolding he was wishing honest Paul Talkebarth at Jericho, and the servants were uttering general lamentations. Albert briefly told his friend of Paul's exploit in the yard. "That old Eulenspiegel is always playing such tricks," said Victor, angrily, "and yet the rascal means so well from the very bottom of his heart, that one cannot attack him."

At that moment all became quiet without; the chief

17

maid-servant had brought the glad intelligence that Hans Gucklick had been frightened indeed, but had come off free from other harm, and was now eating with a good appetite.

The baron entered with a cheerful mien, and repeated, in a tone of satisfaction, that Hans Gucklick had been spared from that wild, life-disregarding Paul Talkebarth. At the same time he took occasion to expatiate at great length, and from an agricultural point of view, the utility of extending the breeding of poultry. This Hans Gucklick, who had only been very frightened, and had not been otherwise hurt, was the old cock, who was highly prized, and had been for years the pride and ornament of the whole poultry-yard.

The baroness now made her re-appearance, but it was only to arm herself with a great bunch of keys, which she took out of a cupboard. Quickly she hurried off, and Albert could hear both her and the housekeeper clattering and rattling up stairs and down stairs, accompanied by the shrill voices of the maid-servants who were called, and the pleasant music of pestles and mortars and graters, which ascended from the kitchen. "Good heavens!" thought Albert. "If the general had marched in with the whole of the head-quarters, there could not have been more noise than has been occasioned by my unlucky cup of mulled wine."

The baron, who had wandered from the breeding of poultry to hunting, had not quite got to the end of a very complicated story of a fine deer which he had seen, and had not shot, when the baroness entered the room, followed by no less a person than Paul Talkebarth, who bore the mulled wine in a handsome porcelain vessel. "Bring it all here, good Paul," said the baroness, very kindly. Whereupon Paul replied, with an indescribably sweet, "A fu zerpir (a vous servir), madame." The manes of the victims in the yard seemed to be appeased, and all seemed forgiven.

Now, at last, they all sat down quietly together. The baroness, after she had handed the cup to the visiter, began to knit a monstrous worsted stocking, and the baron took occasion to enlarge upon the species of knitting which was designed to be worn while hunting. During his discourse he seized the vessel, that he also might take a cup. "Ernest!" cried the baroness to him, in an angry tone. He at once desisted from his purpose, and slunk to the cupboard, where he quietly refreshed himself with a glass of Schnapps. Albert availed himself of the moment to put a stop to the baron's tedious disquisitions, by urgently asking his friend how he was going on. Victor was of opinion that there was plenty of time to say, in two words, what had happened to him since their separation, and that he could not expect to hear from Albert's lips all the mighty occurrences of the late portentous period. The baroness assured him, with a smile, that there was nothing prettier than tales of war and murder; while the baron, who had rejoined the party, said that he liked amazingly to hear of battles, when they were very bloody, as they always reminded him of his hunting-parties. He was upon the point of returning to the story of the stag that he did not shoot, but Albert cut him short, and laughing out loud, though with increased displeasure, remarked that, though there was, to be sure, some smart shooting in the chase, it was a comfortable arrangement that the stags, hares, &c., whose blood was at stake, could not return the fire.

Albert felt thoroughly warmed by the beverage which he had drunk, and which he found was excellently made of splendid wine, and his comfortable state of body had a good effect on his mind, completely overcoming the ill-humour which had taken possession of him in this uncomfortable society. He unfolded before Victor's eyes the whole sublime and fearful picture of the awful battle, that at once annihilated all the hopes of the fancied ruler of the world. With the most glowing imagination, he described the invincible, lion-like courage of those battalions who at last stormed the village of Planchenoit, and concluded with the words: "Oh! Victor, Victor! would you had been there, and fought with me!"

Victor had moved close to the baroness's chair, and having picked up the large ball of worsted, which had rolled down from her lap, was playing with it in his hands, so that the industrious knitter was compelled to draw the threads through his fingers, and often could not avoid touching his arm with her long needle.

At the words, which Albert uttered with an elevated voice, Victor appeared suddenly to wake as from a dream. He eyed his friend with a singular smile, and said, in a half-suppressed tone: "Yes, dear Albert, what you say is but too true! Man often implicates himself early in snares, the gordian knot of which death alone forcibly sunders! As for what concerns the raising of the devil in general, the audacious invocation of one's own fearful spirit is the most perilous thing possible. But here every thing sleeps!"

Victor's dark, unintelligible words were a sufficient proof that he had not heard a syllable of all that Albert had said, but had been occupied all the time with dreams, which must have been of a very singular kind.

Albert, as may be supposed, was dumb with amazement. Looking around him he perceived, for the first time, that the master of the house, who with hands folded before him, had sunk against the back of a chair, had dropped his weary head upon his breast, and that the baroness with closed eyes continued to knit mechanically like a piece of clock-work wound up.

Albert sprung up quickly, making a noise as he rose, but at the very same moment the baroness rose also, and approached him with an air, so free, noble, and graceful, that he saw no more of the little, plump, almost comical figure, but thought that the baroness was transformed to another creature. "Pardon the housewife who is employed from break of day, lieutenant-colonel," said she, in a sweet voice, as she grasped Albert's hand, "if in the evening she is unable to resist the effects of fatigue, even though she hears the greatest events recorded in the finest manner. This you must also pardon in the active sportsman. You must certainly be anxious to be alone with your friend and to open your heart to him, and under such circumstances every witness is an incumberance. It will certainly be agreeable to you to take, alone with your friend, the supper which I have served in his apartment."

No proposal could have been more opportune to Albert. He immediately in the most courteous language, wished a good night to his kind hostess, whom he now heartily forgave for the bunch of keys, and the grief about frightened Hans Gucklick, as well as for the stocking-knitting and the nodding.

"Dear Ernest!" cried the baroness, as the friends wished to bid good night to the baron; but as the latter, instead of answering only cried out very plainly: "Huss! Huss! Tyrus! Waldmann! Allons!" and let his head hang on the other side, they tried no more to arouse him from his pleasant dreams.

"Now," said Albert, finding himself alone with Victor for the first time, "tell me how you have fared. But, however, first let us eat a bit, for I am very hungry, and it appears there is something more here than the bread and butter."

The lieutenant-colonel was right, for he found a table elegantly set out with the choicest cold delicacies, the chief ornament of which was a Bayonne ham, and a pasty of red partridges. Paul Talkebarth, when Albert expressed his satisfaction, said, waggishly smiling, that if he had not been present, and had not given Mariane a hint of what it was that the lieutenant-colonel liked, as suppenfink (super-fine)- -but that, nevertheless, he could not forget his aunt Lizzy, who had burned the rice-pudding on his wedding-day, and that he had now been a widower for thirty years, and one could not tell, since marriages were made in heaven, and that Mariane--but that it was the gracious baroness who had given him the best herself, namely, a whole basket of celery for the gentleman. Albert did not know why such an unreasonable quantity of vegetable food should be served, and was highly delighted, when Paul Talkebarth brought the basket, which contained--not celery--but six bottles of the finest vin de Sillery.

While Albert was enjoying himself, Victor narrated how he had come to the estate of the Baron von E----.

The fatigues of the first campaign (1813), which had often proved too much for the strongest constitutions, had ruined Victor's health. The waters at Aix-la-Chapelle would, he hoped, restore him, and he was residing there when Bonaparte's flight from Elba gave the signal for a new and sanguinary contest. When preparations were making for the campaign, Victor received orders from the Residence to join the army on the Lower Rhine, if his health permitted; but fate allowed him no more than a ride of four or five leagues. Just before the gate of the house in which the friends now were, Victor's horse, which had usually been the surest and most fearless animal in the world, and had been tried in the wildest tumults of battle, suddenly took fright, and reared, and Victor fell--to use his own words--like a schoolboy who has mounted a horse for the first time. He lay insensible, while the blood flowed from a severe wound in his head, which he had struck against a sharp stone. He was carried into the house, and here, as removal seemed dangerous, he was forced to remain till the time of his recovery, which did not yet seem complete, since, although the wound had been long healed, he was weakened by the attacks of fever. Victor spoke of the care and attention which the baroness had bestowed upon him in terms of the warmest gratitude.

"Well," cried Albert, laughing aloud, "for this I was not prepared. I thought you were going to tell me something very extraordinary, and now, lo, and behold--don't be offended-- the whole affair seems to turn out a silly sort of story, like those that have been so worn out in a hundred stupid novels, that nobody with decency can have any thing to do with such adventures. The wounded knight is borne into the castle, the mistress of the house tends him, and he becomes a tender Amoroso. For, Victor, that you, in spite of your good taste hitherto, in spite of your whole mode of life, should all of a sudden fall in love with a plump elderly woman, who is homely and domestic to the last degree, that you should play the pining lack-a-daisical youth, who, as somebody says, 'sighs like an oven, and makes songs on his mistress's tears,'- -that, I say, I can only look upon as a sort of disease! The only thing that could excuse you in any way, and put you in a poetical light, would be the Spanish Infanta in the 'Physician of his Honour,'[2] who, meeting a fate similar to yours, fell upon his nose before Donna Menzia's gate, and at last found the beloved one, who unconsciously--"

"Stop!" interrupted Victor, "stop! Don't you think that I see clearly enough, that you take me for a silly dolt? No, no, there is something else--something more mysterious at work. Let us drink!"

The wine, and Albert's lively talk, had produced a

wholesome excitement in Victor, who seemed aroused from a gloomy dream. But when, at last, Albert, raising his full glass, said, "Now, Victor, my dear Infanta, here's a health to Donna Menzia, and may she look like our little pet hostess."-- Victor cried, laughing, "No, no, I cannot bear that you should take me for a fool. I feel quite cheerful, and ready to make a confession to you of every thing! You must, however, submit to hear an entire youthful period of my life, and it is possible that half the night will be taken up by the narrative."

"Begin!" replied Albert, "for I see we have enough wine to cheer up our somewhat sinking spirits. I only wish it was not so confoundedly cold, nor a crime to wake up the good folks of the house."

"Perhaps," said Victor, "Paul Talkebarth may have made some provision." And, indeed, the said Paul, cursing in his well-known French dialect, courteously assured them, that he had cut small and kept excellent wood for firing, which he was ready to kindle at once. "Fortunately," said Victor, "the same thing cannot happen to me here, that happened at a drysalter's at Meaux, where honest Paul lit me a fire that cost, at least, 1200 francs. The good fellow had got hold of Brazilian sandal-wood, hacked it to pieces, and put it on the hearth, so that I looked almost like Andolosia, the famous son of the celebrated Fortunatus, whose cook had to light a fire of spices, because the king forbade him to buy wood. You know," continued Victor, as the fire merrily crackled and flamed up, and Paul Talkebarth had left the room, "you know, my dear friend, Albert, that I began my military career in the guards,

25

at Potsdam; indeed, that is nearly all you know of my younger days, because I never had a special opportunity to talk about them--and, still more, because the picture of those years has been represented to my soul in dim outlines, and did not, until I came here, flame up again in bright colours. My first education, in my father's house, does not even deserve the name of a bad one. I had, in fact, no education at all, but was left entirely to my own inclinations, and these indicated any thing rather than a call to the profession of arms. I felt manifestly impelled towards a scientific culture, which the old magister, who was my appointed tutor, and who only liked to be left in quiet, could not give me. At Potsdam I gained with facility a knowledge of modern languages, while I zealously and successfully pursued those studies that are requisite for an officer. I read, besides, with a kind of mania, all that fell into my hands, without selection or regard to utility; however, as my memory was excellent, I had acquired a mass of historical knowledge, I scarcely knew how. People have since done me the honour to assure me that a poetical spirit dwelled in me, which I myself would not rightly appreciate. Certain it is that the chefs-d'oeuvre of the great poets, of that period, raised me to a state of inspiration of which I had previously no notion. I appeared to myself as another being, developed for the first time into active life. I will only name the 'Sorrows of Werther,' and, more especially, Schiller's 'Robbers.' My fancy received an impulse quite of a different sort from a book, which, for the very reason that it is not finished, gives the mind an impetus that keeps it swinging like a pendulum in constant motion. I mean Schiller's 'Ghostseer.' It may be that the inclination to the mystical and marvellous, which is generally deep-rooted in human nature, was particularly prevalent in me;--whatever was the cause, it is sufficient for me to say that, when I read that book, which seems to contain the exorcising formula belonging to the mightiest black art, a magical kingdom, full of super-terrestrial, or, rather, sub-terrestrial marvels, was opened to me, in which I moved about as a dreamer. Once given to this mood, I eagerly swallowed all that would accord with it, and even works of far less worth did not fail in their effect upon me. Thus the 'Genius,' by Grosse, made a deep impression upon me, and I have the less reason to feel ashamed of this, since the first part, at least, on account of the liveliness of the style and the clear treatment of the subject, produced a sensation through the whole literary world. Many an arrest I was obliged to endure, when upon guard, for being absorbed in such a book, or perhaps only in mystic dreams, I did not hear the call, and was forced to be fetched by the inferior officer. Just at this time chance made me acquainted with a very extraordinary man. It happened on a fine summer evening, when the sun had already sunk, and twilight had already begun, that, according to my custom, I was walking alone in a pleasure ground near Potsdam. I fancied that, from the thicket of a little wood, which lay by the road-side, I could hear plaintive sounds, and some words uttered with energy in a language unknown to me. I thought some one wanted assistance, so I hastened to the spot whence the sounds seemed to proceed, and soon, in the red glimmer of the evening, discovered a large, broad-shouldered figure, enveloped in a common military mantle, and stretched upon the ground. Approaching nearer I recognised, to my astonishment, Major O'Malley of the grenadiers. 'Good heavens!' I exclaimed, 'is this you, major? In this situation? Are you ill? Can I help you?' The major looked at me with a fixed, wild stare, and then said, in a harsh voice, 'What the devil brings you here, lieutenant? What does it matter to you whether I lie here or not? Go back to the town!' Nevertheless, the deadly paleness of O'Malley's face made me suspect that there was something wrong, and I declared that I would not leave him, but would only return to the town in his company. 'Good!' said the major, quite coldly and deliberately, after he had remained silent for some moments, and had endeavoured to raise himself, in which attempt, as it appeared to be attended with difficulty, I assisted him. I perceived now that--as was frequently the case when he went out in the evening--he had nothing but a shirt under the cloak, which was a common commis-mantel as they call it, that he had put on his boots, and that he wore upon his bald head his officer's hat, with broad gold lace. A pistol, which lay on the ground near him, he caught up hastily, and, to conceal it from me, put it into the pocket of his cloak. During the whole way to the town he did not speak a syllable to me, but now and then uttered disjointed phrases in his own language--he was an Irishman by birth--which I did not understand. When he had reached his quarters he pressed my hand, and said, in a tone in which there was something indescribable--something that had never been heard before, and which still echoes in my soul: 'Good night, lieutenant! Heaven guard you, and give you good dreams!' This Major O'Malley was one of the strangest men possible, and if, perhaps, I except a few somewhat eccentric Englishmen, whom I have met, I know no officer in the whole great army to compare in outward appearance with O'Malley. If it be true--as some travellers affirm--that nature nowhere produces such peculiarities as in Ireland, and that, therefore, every family can exhibit the prettiest cabinet pictures, Major O'Malley would justly serve as a prototype for all his nation. Imagine a man strong as a tree, six feet high, whose build could scarcely be called awkward, but none of whose limbs fitted the rest, so that his whole figure seemed huddled together, as in that game where figures are composed of single parts, the numbers on which are decided by the throw of the dice. An aquiline nose, and delicately formed lips would have given a noble appearance to his countenance, but his prominent glassy eyes were almost repulsive, and his black bushy eyebrows had the character of a comic mask. Strangely enough there was something lachrymose in the major's face whenever he laughed, which, by the way, seldom happened, while he seemed to laugh whenever the wildest passion mastered him, and in this laugh there was something so terrific, that the oldest and most stout-hearted fellows would shudder at it. But, however, seldom as Major O'Malley laughed, it was just as seldom that he allowed himself to be carried away by passion. That the major should ever have an uniform to fit him seemed an utter impossibility. The best tailors in the regiment failed utterly when they applied their art to the formless figure of the major; his coat, though cut according to the most accurate measure, fell into unseemly folds, and hung on his body as if placed there to be brushed, while his sword dangled against his legs, and his hat sat upon his head in such a queer fashion that the military schismatic might be recognised a hundred paces off. A thing quite unheard of in those days in which there was so much pedantry in matters of form--O'Malley wore no tail! To be sure a tail could scarcely have been fastened to the few gray locks that curled at the back of his head, and, with the exception of these, he was perfectly bald. When the major rode, people expected every moment to see him tumble from his horse, when he fought they expected to see him beaten; and yet he was the very best rider and fencer,--in a word, the very best Gymnastiker that could exist.

"This will suffice to give you the picture of a man, whose whole mode of life might be called mysterious, as he now threw away large sums, now seemed in want of assistance, and removed from all the control of superiors, and every restraint of service, could do exactly as he liked. And even that which he did like was so eccentric, or rather so splenetically mad, that one felt uneasy about his sanity. They said that the major, at a certain period, when Potsdam and its environs was the scene of a strange mystification, that even found a place in the history of the day, had played an important part, and still stood in certain relations, which caused the incomprehensibility of his position. A book of very ill-repute, which appeared at the time--it was called 'Excorporations,' if I mistake not,--and which contained the portrait of a man very like the major, increased that belief, and I, struck by the mysterious contents of this book, felt the more inclined to consider O'Malley a sort of Arminian, the more I observed his chimerical, I may almost say supernatural proceedings. He himself gave me additional opportunity to make such observations, for since the evening on which I found him ill, or otherwise overcome, in the wood, he had taken an especial fancy to me, so that it seemed absolutely necessary for him to see me every day. To describe to you the whole peculiarity of this intercourse with the major, to tell you a great deal that seemed to confirm the judgment of the men, who boldly maintained that he had second-sight, and was in compact with the devil, would be superfluous, as you will soon have sufficient knowledge of the awful spirit that was destined to disturb the peace of my life.

"I was on guard at the castle, and there received a visit from my cousin, Captain von T----, who had come with a young officer from Berlin to Potsdam. We were indulging in friendly converse over our wine, when, towards midnight, Major O'Malley entered. 'I thought to find you alone, lieutenant,' said he, casting glances of displeasure at my guests, and he wished to depart at once. The captain then reminded him that they were old acquaintance, and at my request he consented to remain.

"'Your wine,' exclaimed O'Malley, as he tossed down a

bumper, after his usual manner; 'your wine, lieutenant, is the vilest stuff that ever tortured an honest fellow's bowels. Let us see if this is of a better sort.'

"He then took a bottle from the pocket of the cloak which he had drawn over his shirt, and filled the glasses. We pronounced the wine excellent, and considered it to be very fiery Hungarian.

"Somehow or other, I cannot say how, conversation turned upon magical operations, and particularly upon the book of ill report, to which I have already alluded. The captain, especially when he had drunk wine, had a certain scoffing tone, which every one could not endure, and in this tone he began to talk about military exorcisors and wizards, who had done very pretty things at that time, so that even at the present time people revered their power, and made offerings to it. 'Whom do you mean?' cried O'Malley, in a threatening tone; 'whom do you mean, captain? If you mean me, we will put the subject of raising spirits aside; I can show you that I understand the art of conjuring the soul out of the body, and for that art I require no talisman but my sword or a good pistol-barrel.'

"There was nothing the captain desired less than a quarrel with O'Malley. He therefore gave a neat turn to the subject, asserting that he did indeed mean the major, but intended nothing but a jest, which was, perhaps, an ill-timed one. Now, however, he would ask the major in earnest, whether he would not do well by contradicting the silly rumour, that he commanded mysterious powers, and thus, in his own person, check the foolish superstition, which by no means accorded with an age so enlightened. The major leaned completely across the table, rested his head on both his fists, so that his nose was scarcely a span removed from the captain's face, and then said very calmly, staring at him with his prominent eyes: 'Even, friend, if Heaven has not blessed you with a very penetrating intellect, I hope you will be able to see, that it is the silliest conceit, nay, I may say, the most atrocious presumption to believe that with our own spiritual existence every thing is concluded, and that there are no spiritual beings, which, differently endowed from ourselves, often from their own nature alone, make themselves temporary forms, manifest themselves in space and time, and further, aiming at a sort of reaction, can take refuge in the mass of clay, which we call a body. I do not reproach you, captain, for not having read, and for being ignorant of every thing that cannot be learned at a review or on parade, but this I will tell you, that if you had peeped now and then into clever books, and knew Cardanus, Justin Martyr, Lactantius, Cyprian, Clement of Alexandria, Macrobius, Trismegistus, Nollius, Dorneus, Theophrastus, Fludd, William Postel, Mirandola; nay, even the cabalistic Jews, Josephus and Philo, you might have had an inkling of things which are at present above your horizon, and of which you therefore have no right to talk.'

"With these words O'Malley sprang up, and walked up and down with heavy steps, so that the windows and glasses vibrated.

"The captain, somewhat astonished, assured the major,

that although he had the highest esteem for his learning, and did not wish to deny that there were, nay, must be, higher spiritual natures, he was firmly convinced that any communication with an unknown spiritual world was contrary to the very conditions of humanity, and therefore impossible, and that any thing advanced as a proof of the contrary, was based on self-delusion or imposture.

"After the captain had been silent for a few seconds, O'Malley suddenly stood still, and began, 'Captain, or,'-- turning to me,--'lieutenant, do me the favour to sit down and write an epic as noble and as superhumanly great as the Iliad.'

"We both answered, that neither of us would succeed, as neither of us had the Homeric genius. 'Ha! ha!' cried the major, 'mark that, captain! Because your mind is incapable of conceiving and bringing forth the divine; nay, because your nature is not so constituted, that it can even kindle into the knowledge of it, you presume to deny that such things are possible with any one. I tell you, the intercourse with higher spiritual natures depends on a particular psychic organisation. That organisation, like the creative power of poetry, is a gift which the spirit of the universe bestows upon its favourites.'

"I read in the captain's face, that he was on the point of making some satirical reply to the major. To stop this, I took up the conversation myself, and remarked to the major that, as far as I had any knowledge of the subject, the cabalists prescribed certain rules and forms, that intercourse with unknown spiritual beings might be attained. Before the major could reply, the captain, who was heated with wine, sprang from his seat, and said bitterly, 'What is the use of all this talking? You give yourself out as a superior being, major, and want to believe, that because you are made of better stuff than any of us, you command spirits! You must allow me to believe that you are nothing but a besotted dreamer, until you give us some ocular demonstration of your psychic power.'

"The major laughed wildly, and said, 'So, captain, you take me for a common necromancer, a miserable juggler, do you? That accords with your limited view! However, you shall be permitted to take a peep into a dark region of which you have no notion, and which may, perhaps, have a destructive effect upon you. I warn you against it, and would have you reflect, that your mind may not be strong enough to bear many things, which to me would be no more than agreeable pastime.'

"The captain protested that he was quite ready to cope with all the spirits and devils that O'Malley could raise, and we were obliged to give our word of honour to the major that we would meet him at ten o'clock on the night of the autumnal equinox, at the inn near the ---- gate, when we should learn more.

"In the meanwhile it had become clear daylight; the sun was shining through the window. The major then placed himself in the middle of the room, and cried with a voice of thunder, 'Incubus! Incubus! Nehmahmihah Scedim!' He then threw off his cloak, which he had not yet laid aside, and stood in full uniform.

"At that moment I was obliged to leave the room as the guard was getting under arms. When I returned, the major and the captain had both vanished.

"'I only stayed behind,' said the young officer, a good, amiable youth, whom I found alone.--'I only stayed behind to warn you against this major, this fearful man! I will have nothing to do with his fearful secrets, and I only regret that I have given my word to be present at a deed, which will be destructive, perhaps, to us all, and certainly to the captain. You may depend upon it that I am not inclined to believe in the tales that old nurses tell to children; but did you observe that the major successively took eight bottles from his pocket, that seemed scarcely large enough to hold one?--that at last, although he wore nothing but his shirt under his cloak, he suddenly stood attired by invisible hands?' It was, indeed, as the lieutenant had said, and I felt an icy shudder come over me.

"On the appointed day the captain called upon me with my young friend, and at the stroke of ten we were at the inn as we had promised the major. The lieutenant was silent and reserved, but the captain was so much the louder and in high spirits. 'Indeed!' he cried, when it was already half-past ten, and no O'Malley had made his appearance, 'indeed I believe that the conjuror has left us in the lurch with all his spirits and devils!' 'That he has not,' said a voice close behind the captain, and O'Malley was among us without any one having seen how he entered. The laugh, into which the captain was about to break, died away.

"The major, who was dressed as usual in his military cloak, thought that there was time to drink a few glasses of punch before he took us to the place where he designed to fulfill his promise. It would do us good as the night was cold and rough, and we had a tolerably long way to go. We sat down at a table, on which the major had laid some links bound together, and a book.

"'Ho ho!' cried the captain, 'this is your conjuring book is it, major?'

"'Most assuredly,' replied O'Malley, drily.

"The captain seized the book, opened it, and at that moment laughed so immoderately, that we did not know what could have struck him, as being so very ridiculous.

"'Come,' said he, recovering himself with difficulty, 'come, this is too bad! What the devil, major--oh, you want to play your tricks upon us, or have you made some mistake? Only look here, comrades!'

"You may conceive our astonishment, friend Albert, when we saw that the book which the captain held before our eyes, was no other than 'Peplier's French Grammar.' O'Malley took the book out of the captain's hand, put it into the pocket in his cloak, and then said very quietly--indeed his whole demeanour was quiet and milder than usual--'It must be very immaterial to you, captain, of what instruments I make use to fulfill my promise, which only binds me to give you a sensible demonstration of my intercourse with the world of spirits which surrounds us, and which, in fact, comprises the condition of our higher being. Do you think that my power requires such paltry crutches as especial mystical forms, choice of a particular time, a remote awful spot-- things which paltry cabalists are in the habit of employing for their useless experiments? In the open market-place, at every hour, I could show you my power; and when, after you had presumptuously enough challenged me to enter the lists, I chose a particular time, and, as you will perceive, a place that you may think rather awful, I only wished to show a civility to him, who, on this occasion, is to be in some sort your guest. One likes to receive guests in one's best room, and at the most suitable hour.'

"It struck eleven, the major took up the torches, and desired us to follow him.

"He strode so quickly along the high road that we had a difficulty in following him, and when we had reached the toll-house, turned into a footpath on the right, that led to a thick wood of firs. After we had run for nearly an hour, the major stood still, and told us to keep close behind him, as we might otherwise lose ourselves in the thicket of the wood that we now had to enter. We went through the densest bushes, so that one or the other of us was constantly caught by the uniform or the sword, so as to extricate himself with difficulty, until at last we came to an open space. The moonbeams were breaking through the dark clouds, and I perceived the ruins of a large building, into which the major strode. It grew darker and darker; the major desired us to stand still, as he wished to conduct every one of us down singly. He began with the captain, and my turn came next. The major clasped me round, and I was more carried by him than I walked into the depth. 'Stop here,' whispered the major, 'stop here quietly till I have fetched the lieutenant, then my work shall begin.'

"Amid the impenetrable darkness I heard the breathing of a person who stood close by me. 'Is that you, captain?' I exclaimed. 'Certainly it is,' replied the captain, 'have a care, cousin; this will all end in foolish jugglery, but it is a cursed place to which the major has brought us, and I wish we were sitting at a bowl of punch, for my limbs are all trembling with cold, and, if you will have it so, with a certain childish apprehension.'

"It was no better with me than with the captain. The boisterous autumn wind whistled and howled through the walls, and a strange groaning and whispering answered it from below. Scared night birds swept fluttering by us, while a low whining noise seemed to be gliding away close to the ground. Truly both the captain and myself might say of the horrors of our situation the same thing that Cervantes says of Don Quixote, when he passes the portentous night before the adventure with the fulling-mills: 'One less courageous would have lost his presence of mind altogether.' The splashing of some water in the vicinity, and the barking of dogs, showed that we were not far from the leather-manufactory, which is by the river in the neighbourhood of Potsdam. We at last heard some dully sounding steps, which became nearer and nearer until the major cried out close to us: 'Now we are together, and that which we have begun can be completed.' By means of a chemical fire-box he kindled the torches which he had brought with him and stuck them in the ground. They were seven in number. We found that we were in the ruined vault of a cellar. O'Malley ranged us in a half-circle, threw off his cloak and shirt, so that he remained naked to the waist, and opening the book began to read as follows, in a voice that more resembled the dull roaring of a distant beast of prey than the sound of a human being: Monsieur, pretez moi un peu, s'il vous plait, votre canif.--Oui, Monsieur, d'abord--le voila, je vous le rendrai.'

"Come," said Albert, here interrupting his friend, "this is indeed too bad! The dialogue 'On writing,' from Peplier's Grammar, as a formula for exorcism! And you did not laugh out and bring the whole thing to an end at once?"

"I am now," continued Victor, "coming to a moment which I doubt whether I shall succeed in describing. May your fancy only give animation to my words! The major's voice grew more awful, while the wind howled more loudly, and the flickering light of the torches covered the walls with strange forms, that changed as they flitted by. I felt the cold perspiration dripping on my forehead, and forcibly succeeded in preserving my presence of mind, when a cutting tone whistled through the vault, and close before my eyes stood something----"

"How?" cried Albert. "Something! What do you mean, Victor? A frightful form?"

"It sounds absurd," continued Victor, "to talk of 'a formless form,' but I can find no other word to express the hideous something that I saw. It is enough to say that at that moment the horror of hell thrust its pointed ice-dagger into my heart, and I became insensible. At broad mid-day I found myself undressed and lying upon my couch. All the horrors of the night had passed, and I felt quite well and easy. My young friend, the lieutenant, was asleep in the arm-chair. As soon as I stirred he awoke, and testified the greatest joy at finding me in perfect health. From him I learned that as soon as the major had begun his gloomy work, he had closed his eyes, and had endeavoured closely to follow the dialogue from Peplier's Grammar, without regarding any thing else. Notwithstanding all his efforts, a fearful apprehension, hitherto unknown, had gained the mastery over him, though he preserved his consciousness. The frightful whistle, was, he said, followed by wild laughter. He had once involuntarily opened his eyes, and perceived the major, who had again thrown his mantle round him, and was upon the point of taking upon his shoulders the captain, who lay senseless on the ground. 'Take care of your friend,' cried O'Malley to the lieutenant, and giving him a torch, he went up with the captain. The lieutenant then spoke to me, as I stood there immoveable, but it was to no purpose. I seemed quite paralysed, and he had the greatest difficulty in bringing me into the open air. Suddenly the major returned, took me on his shoulders, and carried me away as he had carried the captain before. But what was the horror of the lieutenant, when on leaving the wood, he saw a second O'Malley who was carrying the captain along the broad path! However, silently praying to himself, he got the better of his horror, and followed me, firmly resolved not to

41

quit me, happen what might, till we reached my quarters, where O'Malley set me down and left me, without speaking a word. With the help of my servant,--who even then, was my honest Eulenspiegel, Paul Talkebarth; the lieutenant had brought me into my room, and put me to bed.

"Having concluded this narrative, my young friend implored me, in the most touching manner, to shun all association with the terrible O'Malley. The physician, who had been called in, found the captain in the inn by the gate, where we had assembled, struck speechless by apoplexy. He recovered, indeed, but remained unfit for the service, and was forced to quit it. The major had vanished, having, as the officers said, obtained leave of absence. I was glad that I did not see him again, for a deep indignation had mingled itself with the horror which his dark mode of life occasioned. My cousin's misfortune was the work of O'Malley, and it seemed my duty to take a sanguinary revenge.

"A considerable time had elapsed, and the remembrance of that fatal night grew faint. The occupations required by the service overcame my propensity to mystical dreaming. A book then fell into my hands, the effect of which, on my whole being, seemed perfectly inexplicable, even to myself. I mean that strange story of Cazotte's, which is known in a German translation as 'Teufel Amor' (The Devil Love). My natural bashfulness, nay, a kind of childish timidity, had kept me from the society of ladies, while the particular direction of my mind resisted every ebullition of rude passion. Now, for the first time, was a sensual tendency revealed in me which

I had never suspected. My pulse beat high, a consuming fire coursed through nerves and veins, as I went through those scenes of the most dangerous, nay, most horrible love, which the poet had described in the most glowing colours. I saw, I heard, I was sensible to nothing but the charming Biondetta. I sank under the pleasing torments, like Alvarez----"

"Stop, stop!" interrupted Albert, "I have no very clear remembrance of Cazotte's 'Diable Amoureux;' but, so far as I recollect, the whole story turns upon the circumstance that a young officer of the guards, in the service of the King of Naples, is tempted by a mystical comrade to raise the devil in the ruins of Portici. When he has uttered the formula of exorcism, a hideous camel's head, with a long neck, thrust itself towards him out of a window, and cries, in a horrible voice, 'Che vuoi.' Alvarez--so is the young officer named--commands the spectre to appear in the shape of a spaniel, and then in that of a page. This happens; but the page soon becomes a most charming, amorous girl, and completely entangles the enchanter. How Cazotte's pretty story concludes has quite escaped me."

"That is at present quite immaterial," said Victor; "but you will perhaps be reminded of it by the conclusion to my story. Attribute it to my propensity to the wonderful, and also to something mysterious which I experienced, that Cazotte's tale soon appeared to me a magic mirror, in which I could discern my own fate. Was not O'Malley to me that mystical Dutchman who decoyed Alvarez by his arts?

"The desire which glowed in my heart, of achieving the

terrible adventure of Alvarez, filled me with horror; but even this horror made me tremble with unspeakable delight, such as I had never before known. Often did a wish arise within me, that O'Malley would return and place in my arms the hell-birth, to which my entire self was abandoned, and I could not kill the sinful hope and deep abhorrence which again darted through my heart like a dagger. The strange mood produced by my excited condition remained a mystery to all; they thought I suffered from some morbid state of mind, and sought to cheer me and dissipate my gloomy thoughts. Under the pretext of some service, they sent me to the Residence, where the most brilliant circle was open to me. But if I had always been shy and bashful, society-- especially the approach of ladies--now produced in me absolute repugnance. The most charming only seemed to scoff at Biondetta's image which I bore within me. When I returned to Potsdam, I shunned all association with my comrades, and my favourite abode was the wood--the scene of those frightful events that had nearly cost my poor cousin his life. I stood close by the ruins, and, being impelled by an undefined desire, was on the point of making my way in, through the thick brushwood, when I suddenly saw O'Malley, who walked slowly out, and did not seem to perceive me. My long repressed anger boiled up instantly, I darted upon the major, and told him in few words, that he must fight with me on account of my cousin. 'Be it so at once,' said the major, coldly and gravely, and he threw off his mantle, drew his sword, and at the very first pass struck mine out of my hand with irresistible force and dexterity. 'We will fight with pistols,' cried I, wild with rage, and was about to pick up my sword, when O'Malley held me fast, and said, in a calm mild tone, such as I had scarcely ever heard from him before: 'Do not be a fool, my son! You see that I am your superior in fighting; you could sooner wound the air than me, and I could never prevail on myself to stand in a hostile position to you, to whom I owe my life, and indeed something more.' The major then took me by the arm, and gently drawing me along, proved to me that the captain alone had been the cause of his own misfortune, since, in spite of every warning, he had ventured on things to which he was unequal, and had forced the major to do what he did, by his ill-timed and insulting raillery. I myself cannot tell what a singular magic there was in O'Malley's words, nay, in his whole manner. He not only succeeded in quieting me, but had such an effect upon me, that I involuntarily revealed to him the secret of my internal condition--of the destructive warfare that was carried on within my soul. 'The particular constellation,' said O'Malley, when I had finished, 'which rules over you, my son, has now ordained that a silly book should make you attentive to your own internal being. I call the book silly, because it treats of a goblin that is at once repulsive and without character. What you ascribe to the effect of these licentious images of the poet, is nothing but an impulse towards an union with a spiritual being of another region, which results from your happily constituted organisation. If you had shown more confidence in me, you would have been on a higher grade long ago. However, I will take you as my scholar.' O'Malley now began to make me acquainted with the nature of elementary spirits. I understood little that he said, but all referred to the doctrine of sylphs, undines, salamanders, and gnomes, such as you may find in the dialogues of the Comte de Cabalis. He concluded by prescribing me a particular course of life, and thought that in the course of a year I might obtain my Biondetta, who would certainly not do me the wrong of changing into the incarnate Satan in my arms. With the same ardour as Alvarez, I thought that I should die of impatience in so long a time, and would venture any thing to attain my end sooner. The major remained reflecting in silence for some moments, and then said: 'It is certain that an elementary spirit is seeking your good graces. This may enable you to obtain that in a short time, for which others strive during whole years. I will cast your horoscope. Perhaps your mistress will reveal herself to me. In nine days you shall hear more.' I actually counted the hours, feeling now penetrated by a mysterious delightful hope, and now as if I had involved myself in a dangerous affair. Late in the evening of the ninth day, the major at last entered my room, and desired me to follow him. 'Are we to go to the ruins?' I asked. 'Certainly not,' replied O'Malley, smiling, 'for the work which we now have in hand, we want neither a remote awful spot, nor a terrible exorcism out of Peplier's grammar. Besides, my incubus can have no part in to-day's experiment, which, properly speaking, you undertake, not I.' The major conducted me to his quarters, and there explained to me that the matter was to procure something by means of which my own self might be opened to the elementary spirit, and the latter might have the power of revealing itself to me in the invisible world, and holding intercourse with me. This something was what the Jewish cabalists called 'Teraphim.' He now pushed aside a bookcase, opened the door concealed behind it, and we entered a little vaulted cabinet, in which, besides all sorts of strange unknown utensils, I saw a complete apparatus for chemical--or, as I might almost believe--alchemical experiments. From the glaring charcoal on a small hearth were darting forth little blue flames. Before this hearth I had to sit opposite the major, and to uncover my bosom. I had no sooner done this, than the major, before I was aware of it, scratched me with a lancet under the left breast, and caught in a little vial the few drops of blood that flowed from the slight wound, which I could scarcely feel. He next took a bright plate of metal, polished like a mirror, poured upon it first another vial that contained a reddish liquid, and afterwards the one filled with my blood, and then held the plate close over the charcoal fire. I was seized with deep horror, when I thought I saw a long, pointed, glaring tongue rise serpent-like upon the coals, and greedily lick away the blood from the metallic mirror. The major now told me to look into the fire with a mind firmly fixed. I did so, and soon I seemed to behold, as in a dream, a number of confused forms, flashing through one another on the metal, which the major still held over the charcoal. Suddenly, I felt in my breast, where the major had scratched my skin, such a strong, piercing pain, that I involuntarily shrieked aloud. 'Won! Won!' cried O'Malley at that instant, and, rising from his seat, he placed before me on the hearth a little doll, about two inches long, into which the metal seemed to have formed itself. 'That,' said the major, 'is your Teraphim. The favours of the elementary spirit towards you seem to be more than ordinary. You may now venture on the utmost.' At the major's bidding, I took the little figure, from which, though it looked red-hot, only a genial warmth was streaming, pressed it to the wound, and placed myself before a round mirror, from which the major had withdrawn the covering. 'Force your wishes,' said O'Malley, 'to the greatest intensity, which will not be difficult, as the Teraphim is operating, and utter in the sweetest tone of which you are capable, the word ----.' To tell you the truth, I have forgotten the strange-sounding word, which was spoken by O'Malley. Scarcely had half the syllables passed my lips, than an ugly, madly-distorted face grinned at me spitefully from the mirror. 'In the name of all the devils, whence come you, you accursed dog?' yelled O'Malley behind me. I turned round, and saw my Paul Talkebarth, who was standing in the door-way, and whose handsome face was reflected in the magic mirror. The major, wild with rage, flew at honest Paul; yet, before I could get between them, O'Malley stood close to him, perfectly motionless, and Paul availed himself of the opportunity to make a prolix apology; saying, how he had looked for me, how he had found the door open, how he had walked in, &c. 'Begone, rascal,' said O'Malley at last, in a quieter tone, and when I added, 'Go, good Paul, I

48

will return home directly;' the Eulenspiegel departed quite terrified and confounded.

"I had held the doll fast in my hand, and O'Malley assured me, that it was owing to this circumstance alone, that all our labour had not been in vain. Talkebarth's ill-timed intrusion had, however, delayed the completion of the work for a long time. He advised me to turn off that faithful servant, but this I had not the heart to do. Moreover, he assured me that the elementary spirit which had shown me such favour, was nothing less than a salamander, as indeed, he suspected, when he cast my horoscope and found that Mars stood in the first house. I now come again to moments of which you can have but a slight notion, as words are incapable of describing them. The Devil Amor, Biondetta--all was forgotten; I thought only of my Teraphim. For whole hours I could look at the doll, as it lay on the table before me, and the glow of love that streamed through my veins seemed then, like the heavenly fire of Prometheus, to animate the little figure which grew up as in ardent longing. But this form vanished as soon as I had thought it, and the unspeakable anguish which cut through my heart, was associated with a strange indignation, that impelled me to fling the doll away from me as a miserable ridiculous toy. Yet when I grasped it, an electric shock seemed to dart through all my limbs, and I felt as if a separation from the talisman of love would annihilate me. I will openly confess to you that my passion, although the proper object of it was an elementary spirit, was directed among all sorts of equivocal dreams towards objects in the miserable world that surrounded me, so that my excited fancy made now this, now that lady, the representative of the coy salamander that eluded my embrace. I confessed my wrong, indeed, and entreated my little mystery to pardon my infidelity; but by the declining power of that strange crisis, which had ordinarily moved my inmost soul with glowing love; nay, by a certain unpleasant void, I could plainly feel that I was receding from my object rather than approaching it. And yet the passions of a youth, blooming in full vigour, seemed to deride my mystery and my repugnance. I trembled at the slightest touch of a charming woman, though I found myself red with blushes. Chance conducted me again to the Residence. I saw the Countess von L----, the most charming woman, and the greatest lover of conquests that then shone in the first circles of Berlin. She cast her glances upon me, and the mood in which I then was, naturally rendered it very easy for her to lure me completely into her toils. Nay, she at last induced me to reveal my whole soul, without reserve, to discover my secret, and even to show her the mysterious image that I wore upon my breast."

"And," interrupted Albert, "did she not laugh at you heartily, and call you a besotted youth?"

"Nothing of the sort," continued Victor; "she listened to me with a seriousness which she had not shown on any other occasion, and when I had finished, she implored me, with tears in her eyes, to renounce the diabolical arts of the infamous O'Malley. Taking me by both my hands, and looking at me with an expression of the tenderest love, she spoke of the dark practices of the cabalistic art in a manner so learned and so profound, that I was not a little surprised. But my astonishment reached the highest point, when she called the major the most abandoned, abominable traitor, for trying to lure me into destruction by his black art, when I had saved his life. Weary of existence, and in danger of being crushed to the earth by the deepest ignominy, O'Malley was, it seems, on the point of shooting himself, when I stepped in and prevented the suicide, for which he no longer felt any inclination, as the evil that oppressed him had been averted. The countess concluded by assuring me, that if the major had plunged me into a state of psychic distemper, she would save me, and that the first step to that end would consist in my delivering the little image into her hands. This I did readily, for thus I thought I should, in the most beautiful manner, be freed from a useless torment. The countess would not have been what she really was had she not let a lover pine a long time in vain,--and this course she pursued with me. At last, however, my passion was to be requited. At midnight a confidential servant waited for me at the back door of the palace, and led me through distant passages into an apartment which the god of love seemed to have decorated. There I was to expect the countess. Half overcome by the fumes of the fine scents that wound through the chamber, trembling with love and expectation, I stood in the midst of the room. All at once a glance darted through my soul like a flash of lightning--"

"How!" cried Albert, "a glance, and no eyes! And you saw

nothing? Another formless form!"

"You may find it incomprehensible," said Victor, "but so it was; I could see no form--nothing, and yet I felt the glance deep in my bosom, and a sudden pain quivered at the spot which O'Malley had wounded. At the same moment I perceived upon the chimney-piece my little image, grasped it, darted from the room, commanded the terrified servant, with a threatening gesture, to lead me down, ran home, awakened my man Paul, and had all my things packed up. At the earliest hour of morning I was already on my way back to Potsdam. I had passed several months at the Residence, my comrades were delighted at my unexpected return, and kept me fast the whole day, so that I did not return to my quarters till late at night. I placed the darling image I had recovered upon the table, and, no longer able to resist the effects of fatigue, threw myself on my couch without undressing. Soon a dreamy feeling came over me, as if I were surrounded by a beaming light;--I awoke;--I opened my eyes, and the room was indeed gleaming with magical radiance. But--Oh, Heavens!--on the same table on which I had laid the doll, I perceived a female figure, who, resting her head on her hand, appeared to slumber. I can only tell you that I never dreamed of a more delicate or graceful form--a more lovely face. To give you a notion in words of the strange mysterious magic, which beamed from this lovely figure, I am not able. She wore a silken flame-coloured dress, which, fitting tight to the waist and bosom, reached only to the ancles, exhibiting her delicately formed feet; the lovely arms, which were bare to the shoulders, and seemed both from their colour and form to have been breathed by Titian, were adorned with bracelets; in her brown, somewhat reddish hair, a diamond sparkled."

"Oh!" said Albert, smiling, "thy salamandrine has no very exquisite taste. With reddish brown hair, she dresses in flame-coloured silk."

"Do not jest," continued Victor, "do not jest. I repeat to you that under the influence of a mysterious magic, my breath was stopped. At last a deep sigh escaped my oppressed bosom. She then opened her eyes, raised herself, approached me, and grasped my hand. All the glow of the most ardent love darted like a flash of lightning through my soul, when she gently pressed my hand, and whispered with the sweetest voice,--'Yes, thou hast conquered--thou art my ruler--I am thine!' 'Oh, thou child of the Gods--thou heavenly being!' I cried aloud; and embracing her, I pressed her close to my bosom. But at that instant the creature melted away in my arms."

"How!" said Albert, interrupting his friend, "in Heaven's name, melted away?"

"Melted away," continued Victor, "in my arms. In no other manner can I describe to you my sensation of the incomprehensible disappearance of that lovely being. At the same time the glittering light was extinguished, and I fell, I do not know how, into a profound sleep. When I awoke I held the doll in my hand. I should weary you if I were to tell you more of my strange intercourse with that mysterious being, which now began and lasted for several weeks, than by saying that the visit was repeated every night in the same manner. Much as I strove against it, I could not resist the dreamy situation which came over me, and from which the lovely being awoke me with a kiss. She remained with me longer and longer on every occasion. She said much concerning mysterious things, but I listened more to the sweet melody of her voice, than to the words themselves. Even by day-time I often seemed to feel the warm breath of some being near me; nay, I often heard a whispering, a sighing close by me in society, especially when I spoke with any lady, so that all my thoughts were directed to my lovely mysterious mistress, and I was dumb and lifeless for all surrounding objects. It once happened at a party that a lady bashfully approached me to give me the kiss which I had won at a game of forfeits. But when I bent to her I felt--before my lips had touched hers--a loud kiss upon my mouth, and a soft voice whispered at the same time, 'To me alone do your kisses belong.' Both I and the lady were somewhat alarmed, while the rest of the party thought we had kissed in reality. This kiss I held to be a sign that Aurora--so I called my mysterious mistress--would now for good and all take some living shape, and no more leave me. When the lovely one again appeared to me on the following night, I entreated her in the usual manner, and in the most touching words, such as the ardour of love inspired to complete my happiness, and to be mine for ever in a visible form. She gently extricated herself from my arms, and then said with mild earnestness, 'You know in what manner you became my master. My happiest wish was to belong to you entirely; but the fetters that bind me to the throne to which the race, of which I am one, is subjected, are only half-broken. The stronger, the more potent your sway, so much the freer do I feel from tormenting slavery. Our intercourse will become more and more intimate, and perhaps the goal may be reached before a year has elapsed. Would you, beloved, anticipate the destiny that presides over us, many a sacrifice, many a step, apparently doubtful, might be necessary.' 'No!' I exclaimed, 'for me nothing will be a sacrifice, no step will appear doubtful to obtain thee entirely. I cannot live longer without thee, I am dying of impatience--of unspeakable pain!' Then Aurora embraced me, and whispered in a scarcely audible voice, 'Art thou happy in my arms?' 'There is no other happiness,' I exclaimed, and glowing with love even to madness, I pressed the charming creature to my bosom. I felt living kisses upon my lips, and these very kisses were melodies of heaven, through which I heard the words, 'Couldst thou, to possess me, renounce the happiness of an unknown hereafter?' An icy cold shudder trembled through me, but in the midst of this shudder passion raged still more furiously, and I cried in the involuntary madness of love, 'Without thee there is no happiness!--I renounce--'

"I still believe that I stopped here. 'To-morrow night our compact will be concluded,' whispered Aurora, and I felt that she was about to vanish from my arms. I pressed her to me with greater force, she seemed to struggle in vain, when suddenly--I awoke from deep slumber, thinking of the Devil Amor, and the seductive Biondetta. What I had done in that fatal night fell heavily upon my soul. I thought of that unholy invocation by the horrible O'Malley, of the warnings of my pious young friend. I believed that I was in the toils of the evil one--that I was lost. Torn to the very depth of my soul, I sprang up and hastened into the open air. In the street I was met by the major, who held me fast while he said: 'I congratulate you, lieutenant! To tell you the truth, I scarcely gave you credit for so much courage and resolution; you outstrip your master.' Glowing with rage and shame, incapable of uttering a single word, I freed myself from his grasp and pursued my way. The major laughed behind me, and I could detect the scornful laughter of Satan. In the road near those fatal ruins, I perceived a veiled female form, who, lying under a tree, seemed absorbed in a soliloquy. I approached her cautiously, and overheard the words: 'He is mine, he is mine--Oh! bliss of heaven! Even the last trial he has withstood. If men are capable of such love, what is our wretched existence without it?' You may guess that it was Aurora whom I found. She threw back her veil, and love itself cannot be more charming. The delicate paleness of her cheeks, the glance that was sublimed into the sweetest melancholy, made me tremble with unspeakable pleasure. I felt ashamed of my dark thoughts; yet at the very moment when I wished to throw myself at her feet, she had vanished like a form of mist. At the same time I heard a sound in the hedges, as of one clearing one's throat, and out stepped my honest Eulenspiegel, Paul Talkebarth. 'Whence did the devil bring you, fellow?' I began.

"'No, no,' said he, with that queer smile which you know, 'the devil did not bring me here, but very likely he met me. You went out so early, gracious lieutenant, and had forgotten your pipe and tobacco, and I thought so early in the morning, in the damp air--for my aunt at Genthin used to say--'

"'Hold your tongue, prattle, and give me that,' cried I, as I made him hand me the lighted pipe. Scarcely, however, had we proceeded a few paces, than Paul began again very softly, 'My aunt at Genthin used to say, the Root-mannikin (Wurzelmaennlein) was not to be trusted; indeed, such a chap was no better than an incubus or a chezim, and ended by breaking one's heart. Old coffee Lizzy here in the suburbs--ah, gracious sir, you should only see what fine flowers, and men, and animals she can pour out. Man should help himself as he can, my aunt at Genthin used to say. I was yesterday with Lizzy and took her a little fine mocha. One of us has a heart as well as the rest--Becker's Dolly is a pretty thing, but then there is something so odd about her eyes, so salamander-like'--

"'What is that you say, fellow?' I exclaimed, hastily. Paul was silent, but began again in a few seconds: 'Yes, Lizzy is a good woman after all; she said, after she had looked at the coffee grounds, that there was nothing the matter with Dolly, and that the salamander look about the eyes came from cracknel-baking or the dancing-room; but, at the same time, she advised me to remain single, and told me that a certain good gentleman was in great danger. These salamanders, she said, are the worst sort of things that the devil employs to lure a poor human soul to destruction, because they have certain passions--ah, one must only stand firm and keep God in one's heart--then I myself saw in the coffee grounds Major O'Malley quite like and natural.'

"I bid the fellow hold his tongue, but you may conceive the feelings that were awakened in me at this strange discourse of Paul's, whom I suddenly found initiated into my dark secret, and who so unexpectedly displayed a knowledge of cabalistic matters, for which he was probably indebted to the coffee-prophetess. I passed the most uneasy day I ever had in my life. Paul was not to be got out of the room all that evening, but was constantly returning and finding something to do. When it was near midnight, and he was at last obliged to go, he said softly, as if praying to himself: 'Bear God in thy heart--think of the salvation of thy soul--and thou wilt resist the enticements of Satan.'

"I cannot describe the manner--I may almost say, the fearful manner--in which my soul was moved at these simple words of my servant. All my endeavours to keep myself awake were in vain. I fell into that state of confused dreaming, which I could not look upon as natural, but as the operation of some foreign principle. The magical beaming woke me as usual. Aurora in the full lustre of supernatural beauty, stood before me, and passionately stretched her arms towards me. Nevertheless, Paul's pious words shone in my soul as if written there with letters of fire. 'Depart, thou seductive birth of hell!' I cried, when the terrible O'Malley, now of a gigantic stature, rose before me, and piercing me with eyes, from which an infernal fire was flashing, howled out: 'Resist not--poor atom of humanity. Thou hast become ours!' My courage could have withstood the frightful aspect of the most hideous spectre, but I lost my senses at the sight of O'Malley, and fell to the ground.

"A loud report awoke me from this state of stupefaction. I felt myself held by the arms of a man, and struggled with all the force of despair, to free myself. 'Gracious lieutenant, it is I,' said a voice in my ears. It was honest Paul who endeavoured to raise me from the ground. I let him have his own way. He would not at first tell me plainly how all had happened, but he at last assured me, with a mysterious smile, that he knew better to what unholy acquaintance the major had lured me, than I could suspect. The old pious Lizzy had revealed every thing to him. He had not gone to sleep the night before, but had well loaded his gun, and had watched at the door. When he had heard me cry aloud and fall to the ground, he had, although his courage failed him a little, burst open the door and entered. 'There,' he continued in his mad way, 'there stood Major O'Malley before me, as frightful to look upon as in the cup of coffee. He grinned at me hideously, but I did not allow myself to be stirred from my purpose and said: 'If, gracious major, you are the devil, pardon me for stepping boldly up to you as a pious Christian and saying to you: 'Avaunt, thou cursed Satan-Major, I command thee in the name of the Lord. Begone, or I will fire!' The major would not give way, but kept on grinning at me, and began to abuse me. I then cried, 'Shall I fire?--shall I fire? and when he persisted in keeping his place I fired in reality. But all had vanished--both Major Satan and Mam'sell Belzebub had departed through the wall!'

"The continued strain upon the mind during the period that had just passed, together with the last frightful moments, threw me upon a tedious sick-bed. When I recovered I left Potsdam, without seeing any more of O'Malley, whose further fate has remained unknown to me. The image of those portentous days grew fainter and fainter, and at last vanished all together, so that I recovered perfect freedom of mind, until here--"

"Well," asked Albert, with the greatest curiosity and astonishment, "do you mean to say you have lost your freedom again here? I cannot conceive, why here--"

"Oh," said Victor, interrupting his friend, while his tone became somewhat solemn, "I can explain all in two words. In the sleepless nights of the illness, I endured here, all the dreams of that noblest and most terrible period of my life were revived. It was my glowing passion itself, that assumed a form--Aurora--she again appeared to me--glorified--purified in the fire of Heaven;--no devilish O'Malley has further power over her--Aurora is--the baroness!"

"How! what!" cried Albert, shrinking with horror. Then he muttered to himself, "The little plump housewife with the great bunch of keys--she an elementary spirit!--she a salamander!"--and he felt a difficulty in suppressing his laughter.

"In the figure," continued Victor, "there is no longer any

trace of resemblance to be found, that is to say, in ordinary life; but the mysterious fire that flashes from her eyes,--the pressure of her hand."--

"You have been very ill," said Albert, gravely, "for the wound you received in your head was serious enough to put your life in peril; but now I find you are so far recovered that you will be able to go with me. From the very bottom of my heart I implore you, my dear,--my beloved friend, to leave this place, and accompany me to-morrow to Aix-la-Chapelle."

"I certainly do not intend to remain here any longer," replied Victor. "so I will go with you; however, let this matter first be cleared up."

The next morning, when Albert woke, Victor told him that a strange, ghostly sort of dream had revealed to him the mysterious word, which O'Malley had taught him, when they prepared the Teraphim. He thought that he would make use of it for the last time. Albert shook his head doubtfully, and caused every thing to be got ready for a speedy departure, while Paul Talkebarth evinced the most joyful activity by all sorts of mad expressions. "Zackermanthoe," he muttered to himself in Albert's hearing, "It is a good thing that the devil Bear fetched the Irish devil Foot long ago, otherwise there would have been something wrong now."

Victor, as he had wished, found the baroness alone in her room, occupied with some domestic work. He told her that he was now at last about to quit the house, where he had enjoyed such noble hospitality. The baroness assured him that she had never entertained a friend more dear to her. Victor then took her hand, and asked her if she were ever at Potsdam, and knew a certain Irish Major. "Victor," said the baroness interrupting him hastily, "we shall part to-day, we shall never see each other again; nay, we must not. A dark veil hangs over my life. Let it suffice if I tell you that a fearful destiny condemns me always to appear a different being from the one which I really am. In the hateful position in which you have found me, and which causes me spiritual torments, which my bodily health seems to belie, I am atoning for a heavy fault--yet no more--farewell!" Upon this, Victor cried with a loud voice: "Nehelmiahmiheal!" and the baroness, with a shriek of horror, fell senseless to the ground. Victor under the influence of a storm of strange feelings, and quite beside himself could scarcely summon resolution enough to ring the bell. However, having done this, he rushed from the chamber. "At once,--let us leave at once!" he cried to his friend, and told him in a few words what had happened. Both leaped upon the horses that had been brought for them, and rode off without waiting for the return of the baron, who had gone out hunting.

Albert's reflections on the ride from Liege to Aix-la-Chapelle have already shown, with what profound earnestness, with what noble feeling, he had appreciated the events of that fatal period. On the journey to the Residence, whither the two friends now returned, he succeeded in completely delivering Victor from the dreamy condition into which he had sunk, and while Albert brought to his friend's mind, depicted in the most lively colours, all the monstrous occurrences which the days of the last campaign had brought forth, the latter felt himself animated by the same spirit as that which dwelt in Albert. And although Albert never ventured upon long contradictions or doubts, Victor himself now seemed to look upon his mystical adventure, as nothing but a bad dream.

In the Residence it was natural that the ladies were favourably disposed to the colonel, who was rich, of noble figure, young for the high rank which he held, and who, moreover, was amiability itself. Albert looked upon him as a lucky man, who might choose the fairest for a wife, but Victor observed, very seriously: "Whether it was, that I had been mystified, and, by wicked means, made to serve some unknown end, or whether an evil power really tried to tempt me, this much is certain, that though the past has not cost me my happiness, it has deprived me of the paradise of love. Never can that time return, when I felt the highest earthly felicity, when the ideal of my sweetest, most transporting dreams, nay, love itself, was in my arms. Love and pleasure have vanished, since a horrible mystery deprived me of her, who to my inmost heart was really a higher being, such as I shall not again find upon earth!"

The colonel remained unmarried.

J. O.

[The end]